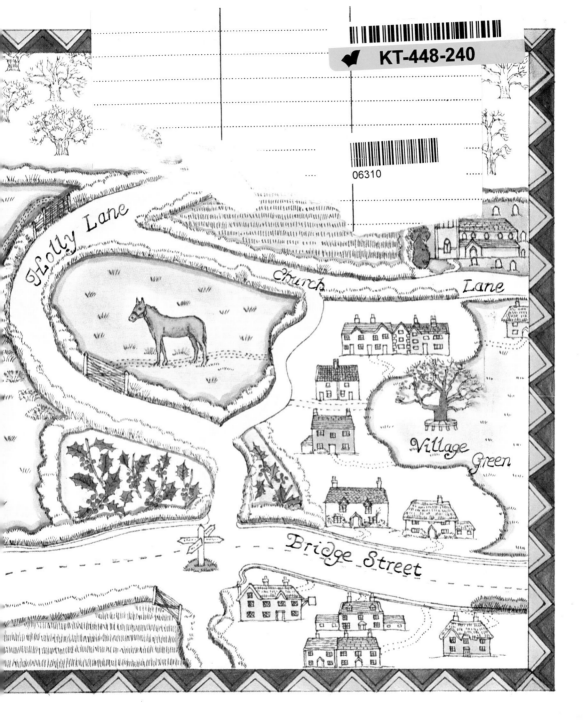

APPLEBURY TALES

COWSLIP MEADOW

By OCTAVIA WILLIAMS *and*
CATHERINE BRADBURY

GRAFTON BOOKS
A Division of the Collins Publishing Group

LONDON GLASGOW
TORONTO SYDNEY AUCKLAND

Grafton Books
A Division of the Collins Publishing Group
8 Grafton Street, London W1X 3LA

Published by Grafton Books 1986

British Library Cataloguing in Publication Data
Bradbury, Catherine
   Cowslip meadow.—(Applebury Tales)
   1. Meadow flora—Great Britain—Juvenile
   literature   2. Meadow fauna—Great Britain—
   Juvenile literature
   I. Title   II. Williams, Octavia   III. Series
   574.941   QH137
   ISBN 0-246-12929-8

Typeset by Columns of Reading
Printed in Spain by Graficas Reunidas

Day after day it had been warm and clear in the village of Applebury. Mark and Clare Burton spent every day of the Easter holidays by Willow Pool or in the meadow. Today they had taken a picnic to the meadow.

Cowslip Meadow only just lived up to its name. Once the field had been a thick carpet of yellow flowers. Now there were only little patches of colour in the grass.

'It ought really to be called rabbit meadow,' said Mark. 'There are so many of them.'

'I know,' said Clare. 'And they're so sweet. I wish we could catch one and take it home.'

'Don't be silly,' said Mark. 'They are wild. They're much better off in their own home. They don't need you bossing them about!'

The rabbits lived in a warren near the top of the sloping field. You could see where the tunnels were from the entrances which were under a clump of hawthorn bushes. 'Look, there are some rabbits,' said Mark, running towards the warren.

'Stop!' said Clare, picking up some grass and throwing it in the air.

'Why are you doing that?' asked Mark.

'I'm seeing which way the wind is blowing, silly,' said his sister. 'You have to make sure the wind blows from the rabbits to us, so they won't smell us. And you must keep still – and quiet. All you ever do is frighten them away.'

'Know-all!' muttered Mark under his breath. And he knelt down to look for caterpillars in the grass.

'Careful!' yelled Clare. But it was too late. Mark had
knelt on a spiky thistle. He let out a yelp of pain as the
spines dug into his knees.
'Never mind,' said Clare. 'Let's have an apple. You won't
find caterpillars yet anyway.'
'Let's give the rabbits our apple cores,' said Mark when
they had finished eating them.

Trying not to disturb the rabbits who were munching at the grass, the children crept towards the warren.
'Look,' whispered Clare, 'there are some babies.' Keeping even more quiet, the two got down on their stomachs and wriggled towards the little fluffy creatures. Just then an older rabbit came out of the bushes. It noticed the children immediately and thumped the ground hard with its hind legs. The babies instantly fled back to the burrows.

'That thumping must have been a warning,' said Mark.
'Yes,' said Clare, 'it must be more difficult than I thought
to hide our smell.'

They left their apple cores at an entrance to the warren
and then went far enough away not to be seen or smelt.

Soon the older rabbit peeked out of the warren again, checking that the danger had passed. And out came the babies. The older rabbit gnawed at the apple cores and soon several more rabbits appeared. Clare and Mark lay in the grass watching them and the bees that buzzed in the cowslips.

Clare picked some cowslips for her mother. 'Aren't they pretty!' she said. 'They'll look lovely on the sideboard.'
'You shouldn't pick wild flowers,' said Mark.
'You're one to talk,' said Clare. 'You're always bringing home things you've caught.'

On the way home they met Mr Kent the farmer.
'What are those you've got there?' asked Mr Kent, pointing to the wilting flowers in Clare's hand.
'Cowslips for mum,' smiled Clare.
'Don't you know, young lady, that it's wrong to pick wild flowers. No wonder there are so few cowslips left.'
'Told you so,' said Mark, under his breath. Poor Clare burst into tears and ran all the way home.

The children were back at school before it was time to collect caterpillars, and the baby rabbits were growing fast. Mr Kent, who owned the meadow, really didn't like the rabbits; they ate the grass his cows liked to eat. When Clare found two dead rabbits she was sure Mr Kent had killed them. She decided to watch him.

Mark was more interested in caterpillars. The nettles were covered with them.

One Saturday he set off to collect some. Clare followed him and arrived in Cowslip Meadow just in time to see him blunder into a clump of nettles. He was stung all the way up to his knees.

Clare collected some dock leaves and gave them to Mark to soothe the stings on his legs. Neither of them knew whether it did any good but people said that was why nettles and docks grew side by side.

Clare had a plastic bag with her, full of carrots and lettuce for the rabbits. She emptied it and gave it to Mark so that he could pick the nettles without being stung again.

His legs were still stinging as he carried his caterpillars home.

His mum found him a big jar and helped him make a
house for the caterpillars.

Clare couldn't quite work out why it was okay for Mark
to pick nettles while she got told off for picking cowslips,
but she didn't complain. She enjoyed watching the
caterpillars grow.

They grew and grew. During the next few weeks Mark changed the nettles every day so that the caterpillars had fresh food. Then the caterpillars stopped eating. They simply hung upside down from a withering stem and gradually, before the family's eyes, they changed shape into chrysalids.

Several weeks later two beautiful small tortoiseshell butterflies emerged and Mark took them back to Cowslip Meadow.

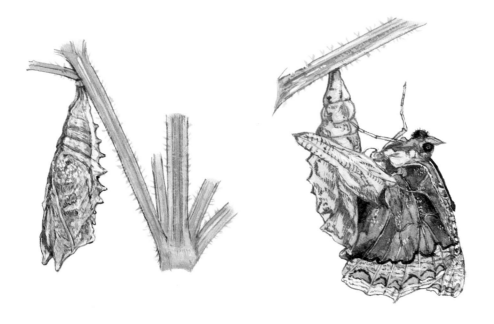

It was a hot sunny August day. The children took a picnic
and ate it as they watched the rabbits and wondered
which of the butterflies were theirs. There were lots of
small tortoiseshells in the field feeding on the thistles and
other flowers that were now in bloom. As they lazed in
the grass a mole suddenly emerged from its hole, shaking
the soil from its nose. There were lots of molehills in the
meadow. Clare and Mark set off to count them. There
were more than a hundred of them just in one corner of
the meadow.

It was late afternoon when they came back to get their picnic things. Clare went ahead to get them.
'Ugh!' she screamed when she reached the picnic bag.
'Help! There are flying ants everywhere.'
They got in her hair and flew in her face. She dropped the bag and ran. Mark picked it up, and raced after her.

The two children ran all the way to the village. The ants were swarming there too.
'Oh! Mr Kent,' said Clare to the farmer, who was chatting to her mother, 'aren't they disgusting!'
'No, it's quite natural. It's just the ants' wedding day.'
'Yes,' said Mrs Burton. 'It happens every year. We get a really hot day and the ants come out to mate.'

Soon the tall grasses began to grow brown and clouds of
thistledown blew over the meadow. Clare and Mark went
back to school again but they still went to the meadow
each day to look at the rabbits. Sometimes there was a
dead one and both the children were upset. Once they
saw a vole being killed by a kestrel. The bird hovered up
in the sky and then suddenly dropped like a stone and
flew up with the tiny animal in its claws.
'That must be what's killing the rabbits,' said Mark to Mr
Kent.

'More likely it's the stoats,' said Mr Kent, pointing to three slim brown animals romping on the grass. 'They've got vicious little teeth and they like a nice rabbit to eat, thank goodness.'

'Oh dear,' said Clare, 'I thought it was you who killed them.'

'I'm sorry I was so rude,' Clare told Mr Kent that evening when he came to visit them. 'You seem to care so much more about cowslips than rabbits.'
'Well, we need to keep the rabbits under control. I don't want to lose my living,' he said.

'Talking of control though, young lady,' smiled Mr Kent, 'your mother and I reckoned you might be able to control this.' And out of his bag he took a tiny rabbit.
'My tame rabbit had babies a few weeks ago,' he said, 'and I promised your mother I'd bring you one. As it is your birthday tomorrow, I've brought it now.'

Clare hugged Mr Kent and her mother and even Mark. She was overjoyed. At last, she'd got a pet of her own. 'I'll call him Cowslip,' she said, 'and I'll get Dad to build him a hutch.'

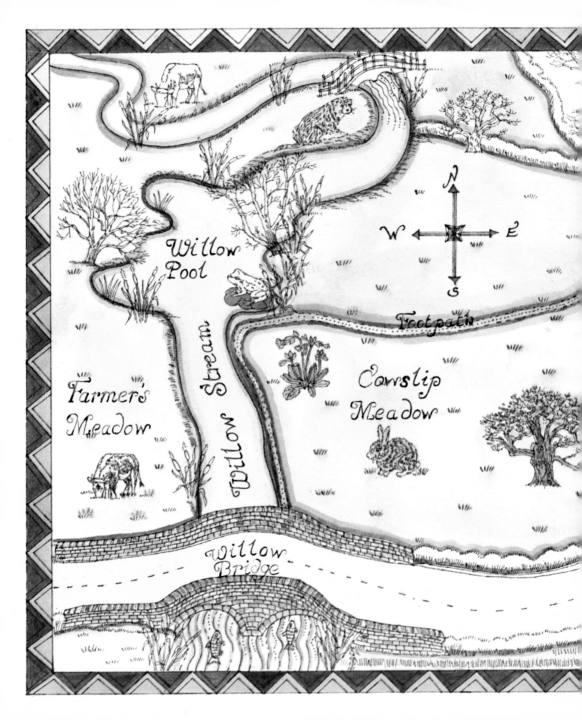

Willow Pool

Farmer's Meadow

Willow Stream

Cowslip Meadow

Footpath

Willow Bridge

N
W   E
S